NATASHA WING'S
The Night Before
Kwanzaa

Grosset & Dunlap

For those who celebrate Kwanzaa,
and for Kirsti Jewel, much thanks—NW

To my lifelong friend, Jamaal,
who taught me about Kwanzaa when
we were in kindergarten—KJ

To all who celebrate: Kwanzaa yenu iwe na heri—AW

GROSSET & DUNLAP
An imprint of Penguin Random House LLC, New York

First published in the United States of America by Grosset & Dunlap,
an imprint of Penguin Random House LLC, New York, 2023

Visit us online at penguinrandomhouse.com.

Library of Congress Cataloging-in-Publication Data is available.

Manufactured in China

ISBN 9780593519752   10 9 8 7 6 5 4 3 2 1 HH

NATASHA WING'S
The Night Before
Kwanzaa

By Natasha Wing and Kirsti Jewel

Illustrated by Amy Wummer

Grosset & Dunlap

'Twas the night before Kwanzaa,
a Black American holiday.
This year it's extra special
'cause Granny's come to stay.

We'll celebrate Black culture,
of our people, far and near.
It goes from the day after Christmas
through the first of the year.

"See those two ears of corn—
the smaller one's for me.
The other's for my brother,
who I can't wait to see!"

"We put nuts and pears in baskets
to represent harvest fruits."

"And here's the cup of unity,
plus books about our roots."

"This is our kinara.
It holds the candles so bright.
We start with the black one,
then light a new one each night."

Each day we ask "Habari gani?"
to start our family meeting.
It means "What is the news?"
It's a Swahili greeting.

Then we answer in Swahili
the principle word of the day.
A principle is like a theme
that we celebrate our own way.

We are all so excited
because Jamaal texted to say
he got some extra time off!
"He's coming soon! Hooray!"

That night I nestled
all snug in my bed,
while visions of Black heroes
danced in my head.

DAY 1: BLACK CANDLE
Umoja (oo-MOH-jah)
Unity

We gather round the kinara.
The first day is about unity.
Then I light the black candle,
and we speak of our community.

DAY 2: RED CANDLE
Kujichagulia (koo-JEE-cha-GOO-lee-ah)
Self-determination

Today is about telling stories
and speaking up with our voices.
We take charge of our lives
by making our own choices.

DAY 3: GREEN CANDLE
Ujima (oo-JEE-mah)
Responsibility

On this day we work together—
our family's a great team!
We help each other out
and support each other's dream.

DAY 4: RED CANDLE
Ujamaa (oo-JAH-mah)
Cooperative Economics

This morning we go downtown
to browse in local shops.
We show our support by buying
from Black-owned mom-and-pops.

DAY 5: GREEN CANDLE
Nia (NEE-ah)
Purpose

On day five we read books
about heroes and history, too.
I imagine the great things
that I might someday do.

DAY 6: RED CANDLE
Kuumba (koo-OOM-bah)
Creativity

Our friends come to our Karamu Feast!
When they see it, they go, "Wow!"
But why isn't my brother here yet?
I hope he's on the train by now.

We eat smothered ribs and okra,
gumbo and collard greens.
A baked ham with sweet yams,
and hot soup made with beans.

When what to our astonished
eyes should appear
but my brother, Jamaal!
"Hey, everyone! I'm here!"

After dinner I recite a poem
while Granny reads along.

Then Dad beats the drum,
and Jamaal sings a song.

DAY 7: GREEN CANDLE
Imani (ee-MAH-nee)
Faith

On the last day of Kwanzaa,
we talk of faith and Black achievers,
and that we must stay joyful
and be our biggest believers.

I give Granny a present that I made.
"Thank you so much, my dear."
Now she can wear her bracelet
to remember Kwanzaa all year!